DECLUTTERING

THE TRANSITION INTO A TEENAGER

DANIEL MCMAHON

DEDICATION

This book is dedicated to countless teenagers and their families who strive to create harmony in their living spaces amidst the whirlwind of adolescence. To the teens who courageously face the challenges of growing up while seeking order in their environments, may this guide be a source of inspiration and empowerment?

To the parents and guardians who tirelessly nurture their children through this transformative phase, this work is a testament to your patience, love, and commitment. Your efforts to support and guide them as they navigate their journey into adulthood are invaluable.

Finally, to the advocates of mindfulness and minimalism, whose principles have illuminated the path toward simplicity and clarity in an increasingly cluttered world, this book is a tribute to your vision and wisdom. May it contribute to fostering spaces where growth and self-discovery thrive.

ACKNOWLEDGEMENT

Writing this book has been a profoundly enriching journey that would not have been possible without the encouragement and support of many individuals. My heartfelt thanks go to my family, whose unwavering belief in my vision laid this project's foundation.

I am profoundly grateful to my friends and colleagues, who shared their insights, experiences, and expertise, helping to shape the ideas presented here. Their candid feedback and valuable suggestions have been instrumental in refining this work.

Special thanks to educators, psychologists, and minimalism advocates who inspire change in the lives of young people every day. Your work is the cornerstone of this book's mission.

Finally, to my readers, whose curiosity and dedication to personal growth motivate me to write—thank you for allowing me to be part of your journey.

CONTENTS

PROLOGUE

Decluttering is more than just a physical act; it is a journey of self-discovery, growth, and transformation. Decluttering can represent a gateway to clarity and empowerment for teenagers, whose lives are often a whirlwind of emotions, transitions, and new experiences. This book was born from a simple idea: that the spaces we inhabit reflect our inner world, and by organising one, we can influence the other.

Adolescence is a time of change—moving from childhood into young adulthood's exciting yet uncertain realm. As teens begin to forge their identities, their surroundings often mirror their evolving minds. A cluttered room can signify overwhelming emotions, unspoken anxieties, and a lack of direction, while an organized space can provide the structure, peace, and focus needed to thrive.

Through these pages, we will explore the psychological, practical, and emotional dimensions of decluttering during the teenage years. Each chapter is designed to guide parents and teens through the challenges and joys of creating a space that nurtures growth and balance.

As you embark on this journey, remember that decluttering is not about perfection but progress. It's about making choices that align with your values, learning to let go of what no longer serves you, and cultivating habits that pave the way for lifelong success. Whether you're a teen seeking clarity or a parent hoping to support your child's journey, this book is your companion in creating an environment that inspires and uplifts.

CHAPTER 1

UNDERSTANDING THE EMOTIONAL IMPACT OF CLUTTER DURING ADOLESCENCE

Adolescence is a transformative period marked by emotional, mental, and physical changes. It is a time when teenagers begin to carve out their identities, explore independence, and experience a rollercoaster of emotions. In this transition phase, the state of their physical environment—particularly their personal space—can profoundly impact their well-being. Clutter, often overlooked, plays a significant role in shaping teens' emotional and psychological experiences.

1.1 THE PSYCHOLOGICAL EFFECTS OF CLUTTER ON TEENS

Clutter is more than just a mess; it is a source of stress and anxiety. For teenagers who are already navigating hormonal changes and heightened emotional sensitivity, a cluttered environment can exacerbate feelings of being overwhelmed. Studies have shown that clutter increases cortisol levels, the hormone associated with stress, making it harder for individuals to relax and focus.

For teens, their rooms are sanctuaries—a space where they retreat from the world to process emotions, study, and relax. However, when this space is filled with unnecessary items, it can create a sensory overload. This constant visual reminder of disorganisation can lead to frustration and inadequacy. For instance, a teen struggling to complete homework at a cluttered desk may struggle to concentrate, leading to a sense of failure and diminished self-esteem.

Moreover, clutter can affect sleep quality. A messy room can disrupt a teen's ability to unwind, making it harder to fall asleep. Poor sleep, in turn, affects mood, cognitive function, and overall mental health. The cycle of clutter-induced stress becomes a feedback loop, further entrenching negative emotions.

1.2 HOW CHANGING ENVIRONMENTS REFLECT EMOTIONAL TRANSITIONS

As teenagers grow, their needs and interests evolve, and so does their relationship with their physical environment. Childhood toys and memorabilia often lose their appeal, yet many teens struggle to part with these items. This reluctance is not merely about the objects themselves but about what they represent: memories of simpler times, moments of joy, and connections to their younger selves.

A teenager's room often becomes a visual representation of their emotional state. For example, a teen going through a turbulent phase may have a room that mirrors their inner chaos, with items scattered haphazardly. On the other hand, a teen experiencing a period of clarity and purpose might be more inclined to keep their space tidy and organised. The state of their room serves as a reflection of their internal world, providing valuable insights for parents and caregivers.

Changing environments also symbolise the emotional transitions that come with adolescence. Moving from the "little kid" phase to the "young adult" stage is marked by letting go of certain aspects of childhood. This can be both liberating and unsettling. Teens may feel conflicted about discarding items that hold sentimental value while yearning for a space that reflects their current identity.

1.3 PARENTAL PERSPECTIVES: LETTING GO OF THE "LITTLE KID" YEARS

For parents, decluttering a teenager's room can be an emotional journey. Childhood items often hold sentimental value, not just for the teen but also for the parents. Seeing a beloved stuffed animal or a stack of old storybooks can evoke memories of bedtime routines, first words, and cherished moments. Letting go of these items can feel like letting go of the child their teen once was.

This emotional attachment can sometimes lead to resistance when it comes to decluttering. Parents may struggle to balance their feelings with their teen's independence needs. However, it is essential to recognise that holding onto these items may hinder a teen's ability to grow and establish their identity.

Parents can navigate this process by involving their teens in decision-making. Instead of dictating what stays and what goes, parents can encourage their teens to evaluate the importance of each item. This collaborative approach respects the teen's autonomy and helps parents come to terms with the changes in their child's life.

Additionally, parents can focus on creating a supportive environment during the decluttering process. Acknowledging the significance of certain items and validating their teen's feelings can make the experience less daunting. For instance, parents can suggest creating a "memory box" for unique keepsakes if a teen hesitates to part with a childhood trophy. This allows both the parent and the teen to honour the past while making room for the future.

PRACTICAL STRATEGIES FOR EMOTIONAL DECLUTTERING

* **Open Communication:** Start with a conversation about the importance of decluttering and how it can positively impact emotional well-being. Frame it as a collaborative effort rather than a chore.

* **Set Realistic Goals:** Break the process into manageable steps. Focus on one area at a time, such as a desk or closet, to avoid overwhelming the teen.

* **Prioritize Sentimental Items:** Encourage teens to reflect on what truly matters. Help them differentiate between items that hold genuine sentimental value and those that no longer serve a purpose.

* **Model Healthy Habits:** Parents can lead by example by decluttering their spaces. This demonstrates the benefits of organisation and reinforces the importance of letting go.

* **Celebrate Progress:** Acknowledge and celebrate small victories. Completing even a tiny decluttering task can boost a teen's confidence and motivation.

The Path Forward

Decluttering during adolescence is more than tidying up; it is a journey of self-discovery and emotional growth. By addressing the psychological effects of clutter, understanding the symbolism of changing environments, and navigating parental perspectives, families can create spaces that foster mental clarity, resilience, and a sense of ownership. This process is a stepping stone toward independence and a more organised, balanced life for teens.

CHAPTER 2

THE BENEFITS OF A DECLUTTERED SPACE FOR TEEN MENTAL HEALTH

This teenage years are transformative, filled with emotional highs and lows, significant life changes, and evolving personal identities. Amid these challenges, a cluttered space can add unnecessary stress, while a tidy environment can serve as a sanctuary of peace and productivity. This chapter will explore how decluttering can significantly impact teen mental health by reducing stress and anxiety, fostering focus and creativity, and building resilience through organisation.

Decluttering as a Tool to Reduce Stress and Anxiety

Teenagers often experience heightened stress levels due to academic pressures, social dynamics, and hormonal changes. When their personal space is cluttered, it can be a visual reminder of chaos, contributing to overwhelming feelings.

2.1 THE CONNECTION BETWEEN CLUTTER AND ANXIETY

Research has shown that cluttered environments can increase cortisol levels, the hormone associated with stress. This heightened stress can manifest in various ways for teens, such as irritability, difficulty concentrating, or even physical symptoms like headaches and fatigue. A clutter-free space, on the other hand, provides a sense of order and control, which is crucial for their mental well-being.

For example, imagine a teen coming home after a long day of school and extracurricular activities. If their room is messy, with clothes strewn about and school supplies scattered, they may feel frustrated. In contrast, entering a tidy, organised space can evoke a sense of calm, offering a mental reset.

Emotional Weight of Clutter

Clutter often carries emotional weight. Teens may hold onto items reminding them of past relationships, achievements, or failures. While these objects may seem harmless, they can unconsciously anchor teens to emotional states they must move past. By decluttering, they can create space not only in their rooms but also in their minds, fostering emotional clarity.

2.2 PRACTICAL STEPS TO REDUCE STRESS THROUGH DECLUTTERING

To help teens harness the stress-reducing benefits of decluttering, parents and caregivers can guide them through manageable steps:

* **Start Small:** Begin with a single drawer or shelf to avoid overwhelming them.
* **Set Clear Goals:** Define what the decluttering session aims to achieve, such as creating a more functional study area.
* **Incorporate Breaks:** Allow teens to take breaks to avoid fatigue and maintain focus.

How a Tidy Space Fosters Focus, Creativity, and Productivity

A clutter-free environment does more than reduce stress—it actively enhances a teen's ability to focus, think creatively, and be productive.

The Science of Focus

Clutter competes for attention. Neuroscience research suggests that a disorganised space can overstimulate the brain, making it harder to concentrate. This distraction can negatively impact teens' academic performance and extracurricular pursuits. A tidy room, however, minimises distractions and creates an environment conducive to focused work.

For instance, a teen studying for an important exam in a cluttered room might find their eyes wandering to unrelated items, such as unfinished art projects or scattered magazines. Their brain can devote full attention to the task in a clean and organised room.

Creativity in Order

While some may argue that creativity thrives in chaos, a certain order level is essential for sustained creative output. A tidy space allows teens to access their materials easily, brainstorm ideas without interruption, and execute projects efficiently. For example, an organised art station with neatly arranged supplies can inspire a teen to dive into their creative endeavours without the frustration of searching for tools.

Productivity Boost

Productivity is closely tied to the environment. A decluttered space promotes efficiency by reducing the time spent searching for items or reorganising materials. Teens can allocate more energy to their priorities, whether completing homework, practising an instrument, or pursuing a hobby.

2.3 BUILDING RESILIENCE THROUGH THE PROCESS OF ORGANIZATION

Decluttering can teach teens valuable life skills, such as decision-making, problem-solving, and resilience.

Decision-Making Skills

Decluttering requires teens to decide what to keep, donate, or discard. This process encourages critical thinking and helps them develop a sense of ownership over their choices. For instance, deciding whether to keep a childhood toy or pass it on to someone else can teach them to evaluate sentimental value versus practicality.

Problem-Solving Abilities

Organising a space often involves problem-solving. Teens may need to figure out how to maximise storage in a small room or create zones for different activities. These challenges help them develop creative solutions and adapt to constraints, skills that are transferable to other areas of life.

Building Emotional Resilience

Decluttering can be an emotionally charged process, especially when it involves letting go of items with sentimental value. By navigating these emotions, teens learn to cope with discomfort and build emotional resilience. They also experience the rewarding feeling of accomplishment when their efforts result in a clean, functional space.

Tips for Supporting Teens in Decluttering

* **Lead by Example:** Parents can model decluttering behaviours by organising their spaces.
* **Provide Encouragement:** Praise their efforts and highlight the positive outcomes of their decluttering sessions.
* **Offer Tools and Resources:** Provide storage bins, labels, and organisational tools to make the process easier.
* **Create a Routine:** Encourage regular tidying sessions to maintain the benefits of a decluttered space.

Decluttering is more than just a physical act—it's a transformative process that can significantly enhance a teen's mental health. By reducing stress and anxiety, fostering focus and creativity, and building resilience, a tidy space becomes a powerful tool for navigating the challenges of adolescence. With the proper support and guidance, teens can embrace decluttering as a lifelong habit, paving the way for a healthier, more balanced future.

CHAPTER 3

STEP-BY-STEP GUIDE TO DECLUTTERING YOUR TEEN'S ROOM

3.1 BREAKING DOWN THE PROCESS: SORTING, CATEGORIZING, AND LETTING GO

Decluttering a teen's room can seem like a monumental task, but breaking it into smaller, manageable steps can transform the experience from overwhelming to achievable. Here's how to approach it:

* Start with a Vision Begin by setting a clear goal for the decluttering process. What does your teen want their room to feel like? A cosy retreat? A creative space? Involving them in this initial step helps create ownership and sets the tone for the project.

* Create Categories Divide the room into sections—clothing, books, gadgets, sentimental items, and general clutter. Sorting items by category provides structure and prevents the process from becoming chaotic.

❋ Establish Ground Rules Before diving in, agree on some basic rules. For example, if an item hasn't been used in a year, it's a candidate for donation. Empower your teen to make decisions based on practicality and emotional attachment.

❋ Sort Everything Work section by section. Create three piles: "Keep," "Donate," and "Trash." Encourage your teen to reflect on each item's value and purpose.

❋ Focus on One Area at a time rather than tackling the entire room at once; start with a single area, like a desk or closet. Completing one space builds momentum and keeps motivation high.

❋ Embrace the Letting-Go Process. Letting go of possessions can be challenging, especially for teens. Guide them with questions like, "Does this item bring you joy?" or "Does it still serve a purpose in your life?"

3.2 TIPS FOR MAKING THE TASK MANAGEABLE AND EVEN FUN

Decluttering doesn't have to be a dreaded chore. With the right mindset and approach, it can be a rewarding and even enjoyable activity. Here's how:

❋ Set a Decluttering Schedule and avoid burnout by allocating specific times for decluttering sessions. Short, focused intervals—like 20-30 minutes—can make the process less daunting.

* Play Music: Create a playlist of your teen's Favorite songs to keep the energy up. Music can turn a tedious task into a lively and engaging experience.

* Introduce Gamification. Turn decluttering into a game. For example, challenge your teen to find 10 items they no longer need within a set time. Offer small rewards for meeting goals.

* Celebrate Milestones Celebrate small victories, like finishing a drawer or donating a bag of clothes. Positive reinforcement keeps the process enjoyable.

* Incorporate Breaks. Schedule regular breaks to recharge. A quick snack or a moment to relax helps maintain focus and energy.

* Add Personal Touches Encourage your teen to personalise their space during the process. Choosing new decor or rearranging furniture can make decluttering feel like an exciting room makeover.

3.3 PRACTICAL STRATEGIES TO INVOLVE YOUR TEEN IN THE PROCESS

Getting teens actively involved in decluttering fosters responsibility and ensures the space reflects their personality and needs. Here are practical strategies:

* Make It a Collaborative Effort: Instead of taking over, work alongside your teen. Offer guidance but

allow them to make the final decisions about their belongings.

* Start with Their Favorite Area: Begin with a space your teen values, such as their gaming setup or art supplies. Success in these areas builds confidence to tackle more challenging zones.

* Provide the Right Tools: Equip them with boxes, bins, and labels for sorting. Having the right supplies makes the process smoother and more organised.

* Encourage Reflection: Ask open-ended questions like, "What's your favourite memory with this item?" or "Do you see yourself using this in the future?" Reflection helps teens connect emotionally with their belongings.

* Be Patient and Supportive: Teens may resist decluttering, especially when it involves sentimental items. Respect their pace and provide gentle encouragement without pressure.

* Involve Them in Donating: Let your teen choose where to donate items. Knowing their belongings will benefit others, making letting go more straightforward and meaningful.

* Reinforce Positive Habits: Help your teen establish habits to maintain their space after decluttering. For instance, adopting a "one in, one out" rule—for every new item brought in, an old one is donated or discarded—can prevent clutter from accumulating again.

* Make It a Learning Opportunity: Teach organisational skills during the process. Show them how to fold clothes efficiently, arrange books by category, or store items in an accessible way.

By following these steps, tips, and strategies, decluttering a teen's room becomes more than just a task; it's an opportunity for growth, collaboration, and creating a space that supports their mental and emotional well-being. Letting go of clutter allows teens to embrace a more organised and purposeful environment, setting the foundation for lifelong habits.

CHAPTER 4

TEACHING TEENS TO LET GO: SENTIMENTAL ITEMS VS. PRACTICALITY

INTRODUCTION: THE EMOTIONAL LANDSCAPE OF LETTING GO

Transitioning into the teenage years often brings emotions and significant changes. For many teens, decluttering, especially when it involves sentimental items, can feel like a daunting challenge. As they navigate their evolving identities, these objects often serve as tangible links to their childhood, cherished memories, and even a sense of security. This chapter explores how parents and caregivers can guide teens to distinguish between meaningful keepsakes and clutter, make confident decisions, and establish healthy boundaries for sentimental storage.

4.1 HELPING TEENS DIFFERENTIATE BETWEEN MEANINGFUL KEEPSAKES AND CLUTTER

Understanding the Emotional Value

Every object tells a story. A ticket stub from a favourite concert, a childhood stuffed animal, or a handmade birthday card from a best friend holds deep emotional value for teens. However, not all sentimental items are equally meaningful. Helping teens assess what truly matters begins with understanding their emotional attachment.

Relatable Scenario:

A 14-year-old Samantha struggles to let go of a box of art projects from elementary school. Her mother notices that Samantha's room is cluttered, and many items are dusted. When asked why she keeps them, Samantha says, "They remind me of when I was thrilled in third grade." By gently probing, her mother helps her identify which pieces evoke the strongest memories and encourages her to let go of the rest.

Practical Questions to Guide Decisions

To help teens determine whether an item is a meaningful keepsake or clutter, parents can encourage them to ask:

* Does this item bring me joy or comfort when I see it?

* Is this item connected to a memory or person I deeply value?
* Would I notice or miss this item if it were gone?
* Can I preserve the memory in another way, such as a photo or journal entry?

The "Memory Box" Technique

A memory box can be a powerful tool for managing sentimental items. This box—small enough to prevent overstuffing but large enough to store treasured items—provides a dedicated space for keepsakes. Encourage teens to curate their collection by selecting items with the most significant emotional value.

Example:

A 15-year-old Alex keeps his grandfather's pocket watch and a photo album from family vacations in his memory box. Focusing on these meaningful items makes him feel less overwhelmed and more connected to his memories.

4.2 STRATEGIES TO ENCOURAGE DECISION-MAKING WITHOUT PRESSURE

Creating a Judgment-Free Zone

Decluttering is an emotional process; teens need a safe, supportive environment to make decisions. Avoid criticism or impatience, and instead, offer encouragement and empathy.

Case Study:

When Emma's parents insisted that she clean her room, they criticised her for keeping "junk" like old concert tickets and keychains. Feeling judged, Emma refused to let go of anything. Her parents later shifted their approach, sitting with her to understand why certain items mattered. This change in attitude helped Emma feel empowered to declutter at her own pace.

BREAKING THE PROCESS INTO MANAGEABLE STEPS

Decluttering doesn't have to happen all at once. Breaking the task into smaller, manageable steps can make it feel less overwhelming.

Step-by-Step Guide:

* **Start Small:** Focus on a single drawer or shelf.
* **Sort Into Categories:** Create piles for "Keep," "Donate," and "Discard."
* **Celebrate Progress:** Acknowledge and celebrate small wins, like clearing a desk or organising a shelf.
* **Revisit Decisions:** Allow teens to revisit undecided items after a short break.

Using Positive Reinforcement

Praise teens for their efforts and decisions, regardless of how much they let go. Positive reinforcement builds confidence and encourages future decluttering.

Example:

"I'm so proud of how you organised your bookshelf! It looks amazing, and now you have space for your new books."

4.3 SETTING BOUNDARIES FOR SENTIMENTAL STORAGE

Defining Storage Limits

To prevent clutter from creeping back, establish clear boundaries for sentimental storage. This might include:

* Allocating a specific shelf or drawer for keepsakes.
* Setting a limit on the size of the memory box.
* Regularly reviewing and updating the collection.

Practical Tip:

Use clear bins or labelled boxes to store sentimental items. This makes it easier to identify and access them without creating unnecessary mess.

Teaching Organizational Skills

Help teens develop organisational habits that make sentimental storage more functional and sustainable.

Tips for Organizing Keepsakes:

* Group similar items together (e.g., photos, letters, mementoes).
* Use dividers or compartments to keep items neat.
* Label boxes or containers with the contents and dates.
* Balancing Sentimentality and Practicality

Teach teens it's okay to let go of items that no longer serve a purpose. Emphasise that memories are not tied to physical objects but live in their hearts and minds.

Storytelling Element:

Liam, a 16-year-old, had a drawer full of trophies from childhood soccer tournaments. After reflecting on his current interests, he realised he didn't need all the trophies to remember his love for the sport. He kept one special trophy and donated the rest to a local charity.

Empowering Teens to Let Go

Helping teens balance sentimentality and practicality is a valuable life lesson. Parents can empower their teens to create organised, functional spaces that reflect their evolving identities by fostering emotional awareness, offering supportive strategies, and setting clear boundaries. Decluttering sentimental items isn't just about tidying up; it's about teaching teens to cherish what truly matters while confidently letting go of the rest.

CHAPTER 5

CREATING FUNCTIONAL SPACES: STUDY AREAS AND RELAXATION ZONES

INTRODUCTION

The teenage years are a whirlwind of change, from shifting interests to evolving responsibilities. As teens navigate these transitions, their personal spaces often reflect their personalities, priorities, and goals. A room is more than just a place to sleep; it's a sanctuary, a workspace, and a hub for self-expression.

For teenagers, having functional spaces within their rooms can make a difference in their mental well-being and productivity. A well-designed room caters to their need for balance—providing a dedicated area for focused studying and a cosy spot to unwind and recharge. This balance fosters academic success and promotes emotional resilience, creativity, and self-discipline.

Creating these spaces doesn't have to be overwhelming or expensive. With thoughtful planning and creativity, parents and teens can transform any room into an environment that inspires focus and relaxation. This chapter delves into practical strategies to design functional spaces that meet the unique needs of teenagers, exploring everything from adaptable layouts to budget-friendly makeover ideas.

5.1 DESIGNING A ROOM THAT MEETS THE EVOLVING NEEDS OF A TEENAGER

As teenagers grow, so do their interests, hobbies, and responsibilities. A room that once held toy chests and colourful posters may no longer align with their current lifestyle. Designing a room that evolves with them is essential for creating a personal, functional, and inspiring space.

Balancing Personal Expression and Practicality

Teenagers are at a stage where self-expression becomes crucial. Their room often extends their identity, showcasing their favourite colours, interests, and styles. While personal expression is important, practicality cannot be overlooked. A clutter-free and well-organized room can significantly improve their ability to focus and relax.

TO STRIKE THIS BALANCE:

* **Collaborate on Design Choices**: Engage your teen in the decision-making process. Allow them to choose

colours, themes, or decorative items while guiding them toward functional layouts.

* **Focus on Versatile Furniture:** Opt for multi-functional pieces like a bed with built-in storage or a desk that doubles as a vanity. This maximises space while accommodating their evolving needs.

* **Encourage Organization:** Use storage bins, shelves, and labelled containers to create designated spots for everything. A place for every item ensures that the room remains tidy and functional.

Adapting Spaces to Their Changing Interests

A teenager's room should be flexible enough to adapt as their hobbies and goals shift. For example, a teen who enjoys painting today might take up coding or music in a few years. Designing adaptable spaces ensures that their room remains relevant without requiring frequent overhauls.

CONSIDER THESE TIPS FOR ADAPTABILITY:

* **Modular Furniture**: Use furniture that can be rearranged or expanded, like stackable shelves or adjustable desks.

* **Neutral Foundations:** Choose neutral wall colours and large furniture pieces. Add personality through quickly replaceable items like cushions, rugs, or wall art.

* **Create Zones:** Divide the room into zones for different activities—studying, relaxing, and hobbies. These zones can be rearranged as interests evolve.

Making the Most of Small Spaces

Not every teen has a spacious bedroom, but even the smallest rooms can be functional with creative planning. Use vertical space with wall-mounted shelves, loft beds, or hanging organisers. Foldable furniture and hidden storage solutions are also excellent for maximising space without sacrificing style.

5.2 THE IMPORTANCE OF DEDICATED SPACES FOR STUDYING AND UNWINDING

A teenager's room serves as their haven—a place to learn, grow, and recharge. Creating distinct spaces for studying and relaxation is essential to fostering balance and helping teens thrive academically and emotionally.

Psychological Benefits of Separating Study and Relaxation Areas

Combining work and leisure in the same space can blur boundaries, making it harder for teens to focus or fully unwind. A dedicated study area signals the brain that it's time to concentrate, while a designated relaxation zone promotes rest and rejuvenation.

KEY BENEFITS INCLUDE

* **Enhanced Focus:** A tidy, organised study space minimises distractions, allowing teens to concentrate better on their tasks.

* **Stress Reduction:** A designated relaxation area helps teens mentally disconnect from academic pressures.

* **Improved Sleep:** Keeping study materials out of relaxation zones reinforces the room's purpose as a restful sanctuary.

How the Environment Impacts Focus, Stress, and Creativity

The physical environment can significantly influence a teen's mindset. A cluttered desk or an unorganised room can lead to overwhelming feelings, while a thoughtfully designed space can inspire creativity and productivity.

* **Natural Light:** Position study desks near windows to take advantage of natural light, which boosts mood and energy levels.

* **Calming Colors:** Use calming hues like blues and greens in relaxation areas while opting for energising tones like yellow or white in study spaces.

* **Personal Touches:** Encourage teens to personalise their spaces with photos, artwork, or motivational

quotes. These elements make the environment more inviting and reflective of their personality.

Setting Boundaries Between Study and Relaxation Zones

Clear boundaries are crucial to maintaining the balance between work and rest. Simple adjustments can make a big difference:

* **Separate Furniture:** Use different pieces of furniture for studying (like a desk and chair) and relaxing (like a bean bag or sofa).
* **Defined Areas:** Create physical separations using rugs, curtains, or room dividers.
* **Consistent Habits:** Encourage teens to only use the study area for work and the relaxation zone for leisure, reinforcing their purpose.

By thoughtfully designing these spaces, teens can develop habits that foster productivity and relaxation, setting them up for success in school and life.

5.3 EASY AND AFFORDABLE ROOM MAKEOVER IDEAS

Transforming a teen's room into a functional and stylish space doesn't have to break the bank. With creativity and strategic planning, you can achieve a stunning makeover that caters to their evolving needs without overspending.

Budget-Friendly Décor and Furniture Options

Decorating on a budget can still result in a chic and personalised space. Focus on high-impact, low-cost changes that breathe new life into the room:

* **Thrift and Upcycle:** Explore thrift stores or online marketplaces for affordable furniture and décor. A coat of paint or creative DIY work can turn old pieces into trendy additions.
* **Affordable Storage Solutions:** Use stackable bins, hanging organisers, or under-the-bed storage to maximise space without splurging.
* **Wall Enhancements:** Peel-and-stick wallpaper, wall decals, or inexpensive art prints can instantly transform the look of a room.
* **Lighting Makeovers:** Replace standard overhead lights with affordable string lights, desk lamps, or LED strips to create a cosy ambience.

Creative DIY Projects for Personalization

Adding a personal touch to the room through DIY projects saves money and allows teens to express their creativity.

* **Customized Corkboards:** Paint or frame corkboards to match the room's theme, providing a stylish space for pinning notes, photos, or inspiration.
* **Photo Collage Walls:** Print photos and arrange them in a unique layout using string, clips, or washi tape.
* **Repaint Furniture:** Revitalize old desks, shelves, or chairs with a fresh coat of paint in their favourite colour.
* **Fabric Accents:** Sew or glue fabric covers for pillows, lampshades, or bulletin boards to add pops of texture and colour.

Examples of Functional Room Setups

Creating a functional room is all about optimising space while maintaining style. Here are some practical setups:

* **Compact Study Nook:** Use a small desk with shelves above it to save floor space. Add a comfortable chair and task lighting for a focused study area.
* **Cozy Relaxation Corner:** Arrange a bean bag or cushioned chair with a soft throw blanket and a small side table for books or snacks.
* **Multipurpose Loft Bed:** Consider a loft bed with a desk or seating area underneath for smaller rooms to maximise vertical space.

* **Dual-Purpose Zones:** Use a daybed that doubles as seating during the day and a bed at night. Pair it with storage ottomans for extra functionality.

Incorporating Trends Without Overcommitting

Teen styles change quickly, so avoid permanent investments in fleeting trends. Instead, incorporate trendy elements through accessories like throw pillows, rugs, or wall art. These items are easy to swap out when tastes evolve.

By combining thoughtful planning, DIY creativity, and budget-friendly solutions, you can create a room that's functional and a true reflection of your teen's personality.

CHAPTER 6

THE ROLE OF MINIMALISM IN A TEEN'S LIFE

Minimalism is more than a trend; it's a philosophy that emphasises the value of intentionality and simplicity. For teenagers navigating an overwhelming world of social pressures, consumerism, and digital distractions, minimalism offers clarity, freedom, and purpose. This chapter explores how parents can introduce minimalism to teens, its transformative benefits, and how families can model minimalist values in their everyday lives.

6.1 INTRODUCING THE CONCEPT OF MINIMALISM TO TEENS

Minimalism isn't about deprivation; it's about making room for what truly matters. Introducing this concept to teens begins with shifting their perspective on material possessions and helping them define their priorities.

Start by explaining minimalism as a choice to focus on quality over quantity. Discuss how owning fewer things can reduce stress and free up time for meaningful experiences. Use relatable examples, such as how decluttering their room can make finding what they need easier or limiting distractions can help them concentrate on their passions.

Engage your teen in conversations about values. Ask open-ended questions like, "What items in your life make you truly happy?" or "How would your ideal space look and feel?" These discussions can spark their curiosity about minimalism and help them recognise how clutter might impact their lives.

To make minimalism appealing, emphasize its flexibility. Explain that minimalism doesn't have a one-size-fits-all approach. They can start small, focusing on manageable areas, such as decluttering their desk or sorting through clothes they no longer wear. Please encourage them to view minimalism as a tool to design a life that reflects their unique interests and goals.

6.2 BENEFITS OF OWNING LESS: FINANCIAL, MENTAL, AND PHYSICAL

The benefits of minimalism for teenagers extend far beyond a tidy room. It touches every aspect of their well-being, from finances to mental health and physical space.

* Financial Benefits Teens are often at the stage where they're beginning to understand the value of money. By adopting minimalism, they can develop healthy spending habits early. Please encourage them to think

critically about their purchases. Do they need the latest gadget or trendy clothing item? Or could that money be saved for something more meaningful, like a trip, a concert, or an investment in their future?

Minimalism can also help teens distinguish between needs and wants, fostering a sense of gratitude for what they already have. This mindset reduces impulsive spending and teaches them to value quality over quantity—opting for durable, meaningful items rather than cheap, disposable ones.

* Mental Benefits: a cluttered environment often leads to an untidy mind. Minimalism can alleviate overwhelming feelings for teens juggling schoolwork, extracurricular activities, and social lives. A tidy, organised space promotes focus and creativity, making it easier for them to study, relax, and pursue hobbies.

Additionally, letting go of unnecessary possessions can be emotionally liberating. Teens often hold onto items out of guilt or obligation. Teaching them that it's okay to release things that no longer serve them can boost their confidence and decision-making skills. Minimalism encourages self-awareness, helping them identify what truly brings joy and fulfilment.

* Physical Benefits Physical clutter takes up space, and space is a valuable commodity in a teen's room. They can create functional areas for studying, sleeping, and

unwinding by decluttering. This separation of spaces enhances their productivity and sleep quality, contributing to better overall health.

Minimalism also promotes sustainability, an issue many teens are passionate about. By owning less and consuming mindfully, they reduce their environmental footprint, aligning their actions with their values.

6.3 HOW PARENTS CAN MODEL MINIMALISM IN THEIR OWN LIVES

Teenagers are keen observers. They're more likely to embrace minimalism if they see it practised authentically by their parents. Modelling minimalism doesn't mean transforming your home overnight; it's about demonstrating intentional choices and leading by example.

* Simplify Your Own Spaces: Start with your belongings. Declutter your closet, kitchen, or workspace, and involve your teen. Share your thought process as you decide what to keep, donate, or discard. For instance, explain how keeping only what you love and use regularly makes your life easier and more enjoyable.
* Be Mindful with Purchases: Demonstrate mindful consumerism by prioritising quality over quantity. Discuss your decision-making process when buying

something new. For example, explain why you chose a durable, eco-friendly product instead of a cheaper, disposable alternative. Highlight how this aligns with your values and saves money in the long run.

* Prioritize Experiences Over Possessions: One of the most potent ways to model minimalism is by prioritising experiences over material goods. Plan family outings, game nights, or travel adventures, emphasising connection and memories. Show your teen that happiness doesn't come from things but from meaningful experiences and relationships.

* Foster Gratitude and Contentment: Practice gratitude as a family. Regularly reflect on the blessings in your life and encourage your teen to do the same. Gratitude shifts focus from what's lacking to what's abundant, reinforcing the minimalist principle of appreciating what you have.

* Embrace the Journey Together: Minimalism is a journey, not a destination. Share your struggles and successes with your teen, and encourage them to do the same. Celebrate small victories, like decluttering a drawer or resisting an unnecessary purchase, and use setbacks as learning opportunities.

Minimalism allows teens to navigate their lives with greater clarity and purpose. By introducing them to the concept, emphasising its benefits, and modelling it in your own life, you're equipping them with valuable tools to thrive in a complex world. Ultimately, minimalism isn't just about owning less; it's about living more—a lesson that will serve your teen well into adulthood.

CHAPTER 7

ORGANIZING DIGITAL CLUTTER: MANAGING DEVICES AND SOCIAL MEDIA

n today's hyper-connected world, digital clutter is as over-whelming as physical clutter. Teens often face a whirlwind of apps, files, notifications, and social media interactions that can feel suffocating. Organising digital clutter streamlines their online lives and fosters better mental health and productivity. This chapter explores strategies to declutter devices, set boundaries with screen time, and encourage a balanced digital life.

7.1 DECLUTTERING APPS, FILES, AND SOCIAL MEDIA ACCOUNTS

Teens frequently download apps they barely use, keep files they no longer need and follow accounts that add no value. Tackling this digital clutter is vital to reclaiming control over their online environment.

STEP 1: APP CLEANUP

* **Audit Installed Apps:** Encourage teens to review every app on their devices. For each app, ask: "Do I use this? Does it add value to my life?"
* **Delete Unused Apps:** Removing outdated or unused apps frees up storage and reduces distractions.
* **Group Essential Apps:** Organize frequently used apps into folders (e.g., "School," "Social," "Fitness"). This reduces the time spent searching and makes navigation more intentional.

STEP 2: FILE ORGANIZATION

* **Sort and Delete:** Guide teens to delete unnecessary photos, documents, and downloads. Use a "Keep, Trash, or Archive" system for faster decision-making.
* **Cloud Storage:** Teach the benefits of storing essential files in the cloud for easy access and backup. Services like Google Drive or Dropbox can be lifesavers during school projects.
* **Naming Conventions:** Encourage naming files descriptively (e.g., "Biology_Project_March2024") to make retrieval easier.

STEP 3: SOCIAL MEDIA DETOX

Unfollow and Unfriend: Suggest unfollowing accounts that evoke negative emotions or provide no meaningful content.

A feed filled with positivity and inspiration can boost mental well-being.

Organise Platforms: Limit the number of active social media accounts to reduce time and mental strain.

Privacy Settings: Educate teens about adjusting privacy settings to maintain a safe online presence.

7.2 SETTING HEALTHY BOUNDARIES WITH SCREEN TIME

Extreme screen time can lead to sleep disruption, anxiety, and difficulty focusing. Teaching teens to set and respect boundaries is crucial for their overall well-being.

The Importance of Time Awareness

Teens may not realise how much time they spend online. Apps like Apple Screen Time or Digital Wellbeing on Android devices can provide insights into daily usage.

STRATEGIES FOR SCREEN TIME MANAGEMENT

* **Establish Tech-Free Zones:** Encourage tech-free spaces like the dining table or bedroom to promote family interaction and better sleep.

- **Set Daily Limits:** Use device settings to set time limits for specific apps or categories (e.g., "No more than 1 hour of TikTok per day").
- **Schedule Breaks:** The Pomodoro Technique isn't just for studying. I suggest teens apply it to screen time, alternating 25 minutes of use with 5 minutes of offline activity.

ALTERNATIVES TO DIGITAL ENTERTAINMENT

Offer ideas for offline activities that teens can enjoy, such as:

- Reading a book.
- Journaling or creative writing.
- Outdoor activities or sports.

Exploring hobbies like painting or playing a musical instrument.

7.3 TEACHING TEENS THE VALUE OF A BALANCED DIGITAL LIFE

A balanced digital life isn't about eliminating technology—it's about using it intentionally and responsibly. Helping teens understand this balance is a lifelong skill.

THE IMPACT OF DIGITAL OVERLOAD

Explain how constant connectivity affects mental and emotional health

* Overstimulation from endless scrolling can increase anxiety.
* Comparison on social media may lower self-esteem.
* Excessive gaming or online chatting can isolate teens from real-life relationships.

ENCOURAGING INTENTIONAL TECH USE

* **Quality Over Quantity:** Emphasize the value of meaningful online interactions and productive app usage over mindless scrolling.
* **Digital Sabbaths:** Introduce the concept of taking one day per week to disconnect from screens entirely. Use the time for family bonding or personal growth activities.
* **Gratitude Journals:** Encourage teens to log the positives they experience offline to appreciate their non-digital life.

MODELING HEALTHY HABITS

Teens often mimic their parent's behaviours. By demonstrating responsible tech use, parents can inspire their children to do the same:

* Avoid checking phones during conversations.
* Share strategies for organising digital clutter.
* Join teens in offline activities to emphasise the importance of balance.

Organising digital clutter is more than just tidying up—it's about regaining control and fostering a healthier relationship with technology. By decluttering apps, managing screen time, and striving for a balanced digital life, teens can reduce stress, enhance focus, and cultivate meaningful online and offline experiences. This chapter equips teens and their families with practical tools to thrive in the digital age, ensuring that technology serves them—not the other way around.

CHAPTER 8

INVOLVING FAMILY: DECLUTTERING AS A TEAM ACTIVITY

Decluttering can be a deeply personal process but presents a unique opportunity to unite families. By engaging parents, siblings, and extended family members, decluttering becomes more than a task; it transforms into a bonding activity that strengthens relationships, fosters teamwork, and creates lasting memories. This chapter explores how families can collaborate effectively in decluttering, build stronger connections through shared efforts, and turn this practice into a meaningful family tradition.

8.1 HOW PARENTS AND SIBLINGS CAN WORK TOGETHER TO DECLUTTER

Decluttering a household is no small feat, but it's far easier and more rewarding when the entire family works as a team. Here are practical strategies to involve every family member:

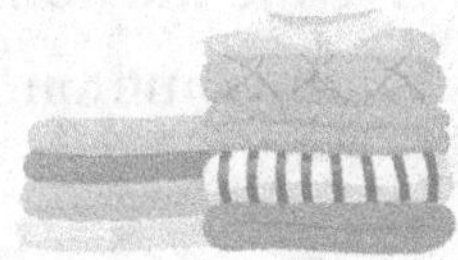

Set Shared Goals

Before decluttering, sit down as a family and discuss your goals. Perhaps you want to create more space for family activities, reduce stress caused by a cluttered environment, or donate unused items to charity. Aligning on a shared purpose will provide motivation and ensure everyone feels invested in the process.

Assign Roles Based on Strengths

Each family member brings unique skills and preferences to the table. Assign tasks based on these strengths to make the process more efficient and enjoyable. For example:

* **Parents:** Oversee logistics, like scheduling donation pickups or managing storage solutions.
* **Teens:** Sort their belongings, including clothes, books, and digital clutter.
* **Younger Kids:** Help identify toys they no longer play with and organise what remains.
* **Everyone:** Participate in group tasks like cleaning shared spaces or moving large items.

Create a Systematic Approach

Divide the home into zones and tackle one area at a time. Start with common spaces like the living room or kitchen to build momentum before moving to personal spaces. Use clear categories such as "keep," "donate," "sell," and "trash" to streamline decision-making.

Celebrate Small Wins

Acknowledge and celebrate progress as you go. Completing a room or even a single drawer deserves recognition. Consider rewarding the family with a fun activity, like a movie night or a special meal, to reinforce the positive impact of your collective efforts.

8.2 BUILDING STRONGER FAMILY BONDS THROUGH SHARED ACTIVITIES

Decluttering isn't just about tidying up; it's a chance to connect with your loved ones on a deeper level. By working together, families can:

Strengthen Communication

Decluttering often involves discussions about what to keep and let go of. These conversations teach compromise, active listening, and decision-making skills. Parents can model empathy and understanding while children learn to express their opinions respectfully.

Foster Teamwork

When everyone works toward a common goal, they develop a sense of camaraderie. Siblings who may typically bicker over toys or responsibilities can find common ground by tackling tasks together, like organising a game shelf or folding clothes.

Share Memories

Going through old items often sparks nostalgia. Family members can reminisce about shared experiences, from vacations to milestones. This storytelling makes the process enjoyable and reinforces family identity and traditions.

Build Mutual Respect

Working side by side fosters appreciation for each other's contributions. Children see their parents' effort in maintaining the home, while parents gain insight into their children's evolving interests and priorities.

8.3 MAKING DECLUTTERING A FAMILY TRADITION

To sustain the benefits of decluttering, consider making it a regular family tradition. This practice can evolve into an anticipated event that strengthens family bonds year after year. Here's how to get started:

Choose a Recurring Date

Select a time of year that works for everyone, such as the start of a new school year, spring cleaning, or the holiday season. A consistent schedule ensures that decluttering becomes an ingrained habit rather than an occasional chore.

Create a Festive Atmosphere

Turn decluttering into a celebration by incorporating fun elements:

* Play upbeat music to keep energy levels high.
* Use colourful bins or labels to make sorting enjoyable.
* Offer snacks or breaks with treats to keep spirits up.

Add a Charitable Component

Involve the family in donating items to local charities or community organisations. Encourage children to choose toys or clothes they've outgrown to give to those in need. This teaches compassion and highlights the positive impact of decluttering on others.

Reflect and Reorganize

At the end of each decluttering session, gather as a family to reflect on your progress. Discuss your achievements and how the newly organised spaces will benefit everyone. Take this opportunity to reorganise the spaces, ensuring everyone knows where things belong.

Document the Journey

Capture the before-and-after transformations with photos or videos. Create a family scrapbook or digital album to celebrate your efforts and reflect on your accomplishments over time.

Case Study: The Thompson Family's Decluttering Tradition

The Thompson family, a household of five, turned their annual spring cleaning into a cherished tradition. Each year, they dedicate a weekend to decluttering, starting with a family breakfast where they outline their goals. With assigned tasks and plenty of laughs, they tackle each room together. Over the years, they've noticed a tidier home and a stronger family bond. Their kids, now teenagers, often lead the organisation of their rooms and even help neighbours with decluttering tips.

Decluttering as a family activity offers countless benefits. It transforms a mundane task into an opportunity to connect, collaborate, and create a home environment that reflects shared values. Families can build a legacy of organisation, mindfulness, and mutual support by working together, celebrating progress, and establishing traditions.

CHAPTER 9

MINDFULNESS AND DECLUTTERING: A TEEN'S JOURNEY TO INNER PEACE

In a world of constant noise, distractions, and endless demands for attention, mindfulness has emerged as a beacon of hope—a practice that fosters clarity, focus, and peace. For teenagers whose lives are often marked by academic pressures, social complexities, and the emotional whirlwind of adolescence, mindfulness can serve as both a sanctuary and a tool for self-discovery. When paired with the physical act of decluttering, mindfulness becomes even more transformative, offering teens a pathway to inner peace and a deeper understanding of what truly matters.

9.1 CONNECTING MINDFULNESS WITH DECLUTTERING

At its core, mindfulness is being fully present in the moment. It encourages individuals to observe their thoughts, feelings, and surroundings without judgment. On the other hand, decluttering involves assessing one's physical environment and making intentional choices about what to keep and let go. When these two practices intersect, they create a powerful interaction. Mindfulness transforms decluttering from a mundane chore into an intentional act of self-care and reflection.

For teens, mindfulness can help them navigate the emotional hurdles of letting go. Objects often carry sentimental value, evoking memories of childhood or symbolising relationships and achievements. By practising mindfulness, teens can approach these items with curiosity and compassion. They can ask themselves, "Does this item bring me joy?" or "Does it support who I am today and who I want to become?" These mindful questions enable them to make decisions that align with their values and aspirations.

MINDFUL DECLUTTERING IN ACTION

Pause and Reflect: Before beginning the decluttering process, teens can take a moment to centre themselves. A few deep breaths or a short meditation can help ground their emotions and set a positive intention for the task.

One Item at a Time: Encourage teens to pick up each item and examine it mindfully. What memories does it evoke? How does it make them feel? This deliberate approach helps them make thoughtful decisions rather than impulsive ones.

Gratitude and Release: For items that no longer serve a purpose, teens can practice gratitude by acknowledging the object's role in their lives before letting it go. This ritual can transform the act of discarding into one of appreciation and closure.

9.2 HOW TIDYING UP PROMOTES MENTAL CLARITY AND SELF-AWARENESS

A cluttered space often mirrors an untidy mind. For teens, the physical chaos of a messy room can exacerbate feelings of stress, overwhelm, and frustration. Conversely, a tidy and organised environment can serve as a calm and inspiring backdrop for their daily lives. Decluttering is not merely about creating a visually pleasing space; it's about cultivating mental clarity and self-awareness.

THE MENTAL BENEFITS OF DECLUTTERING

* **Reduced Stress:** Clutter can be a visual reminder of unfinished tasks and unmet goals, creating a sense of unease. Clearing away excess items can alleviate this tension, providing a sense of relief and accomplishment.
* **Improved Focus:** A tidy space minimises distractions, allowing teens to concentrate better on their studies, hobbies, and personal goals.
* **Enhanced Emotional Well-being:** Decluttering can be cathartic, allowing teens to process emotions and gain control over their environment.

The Self-Awareness Connection

Through mindful decluttering, teens develop a heightened awareness of their habits, preferences, and priorities. For example, sorting old clothes might reveal a shift in their style, while organising a bookshelf might highlight their evolving interests. These insights can help teens make more intentional choices in other areas, fostering a deeper understanding of who they are and wish to become.

9.3 ENCOURAGING TEENS TO REFLECT ON WHAT TRULY MATTERS

One of the most profound aspects of mindfulness and decluttering is their ability to prompt reflection. As teens sift through their belongings, they are invited to confront questions about identity, values, and aspirations. What do they hold onto, and why? What are they ready to release, and what does that say about their growth?

Prompts for Reflection

* **Identity:** What items in your space reflect who you are today? Are there items that represent a past version of yourself that you've outgrown
* **Values:** Which belongings align with your core values and bring you joy? Are there possessions that feel more like obligations than treasures?

* **Aspirations:** Does your environment support your goals and dreams? How can decluttering help you create a space that inspires you?

FOSTERING A MINDSET OF ABUNDANCE

Decluttering can also teach teens an essential lesson about abundance. Letting go does not mean losing; it creates space for new opportunities, experiences, and growth. By releasing what no longer serves them, teens can embrace the idea that they already have enough and that they are enough.

Practical Exercises for Teens

To make mindfulness and decluttering an engaging and meaningful experience, consider incorporating these activities:

Mindful Visualization: Before starting, teens can close their eyes and visualise their ideal space. How does it look, feel, and function? This exercise helps them set a clear intention and stay motivated.

The "Five-Minute Declutter": Teens can start small by dedicating just five minutes daily to tidying up a specific area. This manageable approach builds momentum and prevents overwhelm.

The Gratitude Journal: Encourage teens to keep a journal where they write about the items they've decided to let go of and why. This practice reinforces mindfulness and helps them process their emotions.

A Journey to Inner Peace

Ultimately, combining mindfulness and decluttering offers teens more than just a clean room; it provides them with tools for navigating life with intention and clarity. By connecting with the present moment, letting go of what no longer serves them, and reflecting on what truly matters, teens can create a harmonious environment that supports their mental, emotional, and spiritual well-being.

This journey to inner peace is not about achieving perfection but embracing the process. As teens learn to align their outer world with their inner values, they discover that the act of decluttering is, in fact, an act of self-love. And in that discovery, they find the profound truth that inner peace is not something to be seen but something to be cultivated—one mindful choice at a time.

CHAPTER 10

MAINTAINING A DECLUTTERED ENVIRONMENT: HABITS FOR LIFELONG SUCCESS

In the journey of creating a tidy and organised space, the challenge isn't just in the act of decluttering but in maintaining the environment over time. Adolescence is a critical stage where habits are formed, and instilling a sense of consistency in teens can set the foundation for a lifetime of organisation and mental clarity. This chapter delves into the importance of consistency, practical strategies for upkeep, and how these practices prepare teens for the responsibilities of adulthood.

10.1 TEACHING TEENS THE IMPORTANCE OF CONSISTENCY

Consistency is the cornerstone of an organised life. For teenagers, maintaining a decluttered environment offers more than just a visually pleasing space—it provides stability amidst the chaos of adolescence. Teaching consistency involves showing teens the direct connection between their surroundings and emotional well-being.

Building the Habit Loop

Habits are formed through repetition and reinforcement. To help teens make tidiness a habit, consider the habit loop framework:

* ❋ **Cue:** Identify triggers that remind them to tidy up. This could be as simple as completing homework or waking up in the morning.
* ❋ **Routine:** Reinforce the act of putting away items, organising their desk, or tidying their bed.
* ❋ **Reward:** Highlight the benefits of their actions, such as feeling accomplished or having a relaxing environment to return to.

Start with small, manageable tasks to help teens see how easy it is to maintain a clean space. For example, folding clothes after laundry day or dedicating five minutes each evening to decluttering their study area can be a great beginning.

THE POWER OF POSITIVE REINFORCEMENT

Acknowledging their efforts can be highly motivating for teens. Praise their work, no matter how small, and emphasise their progress over perfection. For example, if they consistently keep their desk tidy but struggle with their closet, focus on the achievement rather than the shortfall. This builds confidence and fosters a desire to improve.

10.2 PRACTICAL TIPS FOR SUSTAINING A TIDY AND ORGANIZED SPACE

While the initial act of decluttering requires effort, maintaining that order can be simplified with practical strategies. These tips can help teens integrate tidiness into their daily routines without feeling overwhelmed:

DAILY MINI-TIDYING SESSIONS

Encourage teens to dedicate 5-10 minutes daily to tidying their space. This could involve:

* Returning items to their designated spots.
* Clearing their desk of unnecessary papers.
* Quickly scanning the room for out-of-place items.

These mini-sessions prevent clutter from accumulating and make maintaining a clean environment less daunting.

ONE IN, ONE OUT RULE

Introduce the "One In, One Out" rule to prevent clutter from creeping back in. For every new item they bring into their room, they should remove an old or unused one. This keeps possessions at a manageable level and encourages thoughtful consumption.

DECLUTTERING CHECKPOINTS

Schedule regular decluttering sessions—weekly, monthly, or seasonally. Use these checkpoints to reassess items and ensure that only what's necessary and meaningful remains. These sessions can be aligned with natural transitions, such as the start of a new school semester or seasonal changes.

FUNCTIONAL STORAGE SOLUTIONS

Investing in practical storage options can make organisation easier. Encourage teens to:

* Use labelled bins for categorising items.
* Opt for furniture with built-in storage, like beds with drawers.
* Utilize wall-mounted shelves to maximise space efficiency.
* The easier it is for them to store items, the more likely they will do so.

DIGITAL DECLUTTERING

In today's digital age, a teen's clutter isn't limited to physical items. Encourage regular decluttering of their digital devices:

* Organize files and folders on their computers.
* Delete unused apps from their phones.
* Unsubscribe from unnecessary emails.

10.3 HOW DECLUTTERING PREPARES TEENS FOR ADULTHOOD

The skills learned through maintaining a decluttered environment go beyond their teenage years, equipping them for adulthood. Here's how:

Time Management

A tidy space fosters better time management. With an organised environment, teens spend less time searching for misplaced items and more time focusing on their priorities. These habits translate into adulthood, where effective time management becomes crucial for balancing work, relationships, and personal growth.

Financial Awareness

Learning to distinguish between needs and wants during decluttering encourages mindful consumption. Teens begin to appreciate the value of owning less, which can lead to better financial decisions as adults. They'll be less likely to spend impulsively and more likely to prioritise quality over quantity.

Stress Reduction

An organised space contributes to mental clarity, reducing stress and anxiety. Adults with decluttering habits are better equipped to create calming environments in their homes, promoting overall well-being.

Adaptability

Adulthood often involves transitions, from moving into a college dorm to setting up a first apartment. Decluttering and organising enable teens to handle these changes gracefully, creating functional spaces wherever they go.

Self-Discipline

The practice of maintaining a decluttered environment instils self-discipline. Teens learn the value of consistent effort and the rewards of staying organised. This punishment extends to other aspects of their lives, such as academics, career, and personal goals.

MAKING DECLUTTERING A LIFELONG PRACTICE

Maintaining a decluttered environment is more than a one-time effort; it's a lifelong practice. Encourage teens to:

* **Reflect Regularly:** Periodically reassess their space and belongings to ensure everything aligns with their current needs and values.
* **Seek Inspiration:** Look for organisational ideas online or in books to keep the process engaging.

* **Share the Journey:** Collaborate with family and friends in decluttering activities, making it a shared experience rather than a solitary chore.

By embedding these habits early, teens can carry the benefits of decluttering into every stage of their lives, enjoying a sense of clarity, focus, and balance in their personal and professional endeavours.

Maintaining a decluttered environment is more than just keeping things tidy; it's a pathway to personal growth and lifelong success. By teaching teens the importance of consistency, equipping them with practical strategies, and helping them understand the broader benefits, we empower them to build habits that will serve them well for years.

EPILOGUE

As this journey ends, it is essential to remember that decluttering lessons extend far beyond the walls of a teenager's room. The principles of organisation, mindfulness, and intentional living can shape a fulfilling life, regardless of age or circumstance.

For teens, this process is a stepping stone toward independence and self-awareness. The habits they cultivate now will guide them through life's many transitions, from the challenges of college life to the responsibilities of adulthood. By understanding the importance of maintaining a decluttered environment, they gain more than just a tidy space—they develop a mindset of clarity, purpose, and resilience.

For parents, this journey is an opportunity to connect with their children, to support them in navigating the complexities of growing up, and to model the values of simplicity and intentionality. Families can create organised homes and harmonious relationships built on mutual respect and understanding by working together.

As you close this book, take with you the understanding that decluttering is not a one-time event but an ongoing practice. It reflects your values, a commitment to growth, and a celebration of the freedom from letting go of what no longer serves you. Whether creating a serene study area, organising digital files, or reevaluating sentimental possessions, each small step contributes to a life of balance and fulfilment.

The journey of decluttering is ultimately a journey toward self-discovery. Embrace it with an open heart, and may the lessons you've learned here inspire you to create a life—and a space—that genuinely reflects who you are and who you aspire to become.